D1276310

BUCKSKIN BOOKS

6

Buckskin Books

Danger in the Coves

BY FRANCES C. THOMPSON

Illustrated by Lloyd Scott

BUCKSKIN BOOKS

MACMILLAN OF CANADA

TORONTO

Library of Congress Catalog Card No. 63-13666

Reprinted 1966

Printed in Canada by The Bryant Press Limited

CONTENTS

CHAPTER 1

Adventure on the River

David Cameron sat with his father and his little sister Jacqueline, in the inn by the river's edge.

"How much longer before we can go across, Papa?" he asked.

"As soon as the Indians are ready, Davy. They have to wait for the turn of the tide. Paddling a canoe across the St. Lawrence when the ice is breaking up is hard work and they won't go until there is still water." He almost said that it was dangerous work, too, but caught himself in time. There was no sense in frightening the children.

The year was 1845 and Davy, ten, and his sister Jacqueline, eight, had been visiting their French grand-mother on a farm near Lévis on the south shore of the St. Lawrence River because their mother had been ill. They had crossed the frozen river from Que-bec City in a *carriole*, a kind of sleigh, in midwinter when the ice was thick. But now, in early spring, dark patches of water were showing, and they had to return by canoe. If they had not been delayed by bad roads, they might have taken the *Royal Mail*, a larger and safer craft like a row-boat. But the Indians had been ferrying people across in this way for a hundred years and more and Mr. Cameron was not really worried.

In a few minutes, the innkeeper

beckoned and said that the Indians were waiting. Mr. Cameron pulled the toques down around the children's ears and tied their mufflers firmly round their throats. An east wind was blowing and it would be cold on the river.

On the shore, a dug-out canoe was drawn up and two tall Indians stood beside it. Mr. Cameron and the children got in and covered themselves with buffalo robes. Another passenger was already seated and Mr. Cameron nodded to him.

"Monsieur Le Blanc, is it not?" he asked.

The man grunted a reply but paid no more attention to them. He was dark-skinned and had a small, pointed, black beard. Davy thought that he looked stern and a little wicked, like

Crossing the icy St. Lawrence.

the pictures of Satan in his book of Bible stories. And he thought it funny that a man who looked so black should have a name that meant "white". He started to whisper to his father, "I don't like him, Papa," but didn't finish. Monsieur Le Blanc was scowling at him.

The Indians prepared to push off. One of them jumped lightly into the canoe and, sitting on the seat near the bow, pushed his paddle through the slush into the hard sand at the edge of the river. As he did so, the other gave a mighty push from the stern, and, as soon as the canoe was in the water, jumped aboard.

5

"See how quickly and easily he did that, Davy?" Mr. Cameron said. "Nobody can beat these Micmac Indians in handling a canoe. Just watch them."

The men paddled swiftly and surely through the open water near the shore, slowing down as they approached what looked like a solid mass of ice-cakes piled high against each other. If Davy had not been watching closely, he would not have noticed that the Indian in the bow gave a quick flick of his paddle to show the way they should go. There was a little open space between two huge cakes of ice and they paddled through.

The children talked about their adventure. Gradually, the channel between the ice-floes narrowed, until only ice was ahead of them. Davy wondered what would happen next. To his great surprise, he saw the Indian in the bow leap to the ice and felt the canoe being drawn up and pulled forward.

"Papa!" he exclaimed. "They're pulling us up on top of the ice. Look! Oh, Papa, what's going to happen?"

"Wait and see, Davy." His father smiled. "They'll pull us over the top and we'll slide down to open water and go on."

"Papa, I'm scared," Jacqueline said, and she clung to her father with all her might.

"I'm not," Davy said as he wriggled around to see everything that was going on. "This is exciting."

Monsieur Le Blanc frowned. He did not like children. He thought that if people insisted on bringing them on such a journey they should keep them quiet. That boy would upset the canoe yet with his squirming and stretching.

As Mr. Cameron had said, the Indians pulled the canoe across the ice-floe into open water. There were several stretches of ice that had to be crossed in this way and, once, a strong current carried them down-river much farther than they wanted to go. Monsieur Le Blanc shouted at the Indians and cursed them under his breath but they paid no attention to him. They were too busy paddling and trying to get into quiet water. Mr. Cameron knew how treacherous the tides and currents of the St. Lawrence could be, but he kept a confident, smiling face so that the children would feel safe.

After a while, Davy asked rather

anxiously, "Papa, it's taking a long time isn't it?" They had been in the canoe for almost two hours and he was getting cramped and cold.

"Yes, Davy. Remember, I told you that you mustn't expect to get across as fast as in the sleigh." Mr. Cameron was cold and stiff, too, and he wondered if he had been foolish to bring the children home with him when they might have waited until the ice was gone and come across on the ferry. But their mother was better now, and anxious to see them and, since he had to go to Lévis anyway, on business, it seemed the sensible thing to do.

Just then, the Indian in the bow gave a low call that sounded like "Oie" and they could feel the canoe edge into the ice-sheet again.

"What does that mean, Papa?" Davy asked.

"I think it means that we'll soon be there, Davy. I'll be surprised if there isn't quiet water the other side of this. See, we're really very close to shore."

Once again they were hauled over the ice and then came to quiet water. The Indians paddled quickly and they soon reached the landing-place near the market in the Lower Town of Quebec.

As they pulled up on the beach, Davy and his father saw three men lounging against a building across the street. They were rough-looking fellows. They came towards Monsieur Le Blanc as soon as he stepped ashore. When they met, they spoke in low voices and seemed to be arguing about something.

The men were not close enough to be heard distinctly but, once, Mr. Cameron caught the word "pay". At that, he took a closer look at them. One of them seemed very familiar. Where had he seen that hard, bitter face before?

Davy, always curious, walked closer to the group of men while his father helped Jacqueline out of the canoe. One of them turned to look at him. The man's face was dark and scowling. Davy felt it threaten him with something dreadful. "Perhaps he's a crimp," he thought. He hurried back to his father and Jacqueline.

CHAPTER 2

The Timber Coves

Mr. Cameron and the children started walking towards the river road which led to Wolfe's Cove, where they lived.

"Oh!" Jacqueline cried as she made her first steps. "My legs are all pins and needles, Papa."

"So are mine," said Mr. Cameron. "It is from sitting so long in the canoe. But we'll be all right in a minute. Whew! That's a cold wind. It's a good thing it is at our backs and not in our faces."

Jacqueline hopped and skipped to keep up with her father and Davy until she was out of breath.

Once, when she had dropped behind a little and couldn't hear what he said, Davy asked in a low voice, "Papa, do you think those men who met Monsieur Le Blanc might be crimps?"

Davy was afraid of crimps. They were robbers who seized men and sometimes bigger boys to sell to the captains of sailing-ships. During the summer when the ships were in Quebec, many of the captains bought men and big boys to replace the sailors who had run away from their ships when they came to port. The crimps caught their victims in the streets at night, tied them up, and took them in row-boats out to the ships at anchor. Some of the prisoners did not see their families again for years.

"I don't think Monsieur Le Blanc

and those men are crimps," said Mr. Cameron. "They say that many of the crimps are respectable people whom nobody would ever suspect. These men were tough-looking characters."

Davy shivered. He was afraid the crimps might get *him* some day. He said, "But Papa, maybe the crimps pay men like that to do the kidnapping for them. Anyway, that one with the red beard looked as if he would have gone for me quick as a wink, if he had had the chance."

"Oh, come now, Davy. You're imagining things. It's the big lads they're after."

"But I'm big for my age," Davy said.

"Aye, but not big enough. Besides, you know as well as I do it's only in summer we have anything to fear from them. That's when there are never enough sailors to man the ships that take the timber back across the ocean. And that's when a crimp can make a lot of money if he can supply a captain with a crew. But it's men they need, Davy, more than boys, and that fellow was probably looking at someone else. But wait! Was that the one with the blue sash to his jacket?"

"Yes, Papa. Why?"

"Oh, no reason, Davy, no reason at all!" But there was a reason. Someone had pointed that man out to him as one of the hated crimps. Now, why would he be talking to Monsieur Le Blanc? Mr. Cameron was very thoughtful as they stopped to let Jacqueline catch up with them.

"Why are the houses all joined together here, Papa?" she asked as they started off again. They were walking along Champlain Street and she noticed, for the first time, that they looked like one long building.

"I suppose they were built that way to save space," Mr. Cameron answered. "As you can see, this is a very narrow strip of land between the river and the cliffs. Rich people used to live here but when the cholera came they moved to the Upper Town where it wasn't so crowded."

"What's cholera, Papa?" Jacqueline asked.

"It's a disease, Jacqueline, a very bad disease."

"Will I get it?"

"No, not likely. Look!" Mr. Cameron said, changing the subject quickly. "There's a man walking away out on that pier."

They were now almost out of the city, where Champlain Street became the river road, and before them the timber coves stretched as far as they could see. Each cove, or bay, was divided by long piers that jutted out into the water from the gently sloping shore.

"What do you think he's doing, Davy?" Mr. Cameron continued.

"He might be looking to see if the ice has done any damage this winter," Davy answered.

"You're right. It won't be long now till the rafts come in."

"Where do the rafts come from?" Jacqueline asked.

"I know," Davy spoke up. "They come from the Ottawa River and Lake Ontario and ..." he hesitated, then

Davy in the coves.

went on, "and lots of places I can't remember, way off in the forests where
they cut the logs. Raftsmen have to
be very strong and brave, don't they,
Papa?"

"Indeed they do. It's hard to steer
those rafts through the rapids."

Davy liked the spring-time when the

rafts came in and the men went up
and down the river road, singing and
shouting and, sometimes, fighting.
Then the coves would be filled with
the squared logs called "timber", and
there would be strings of "booms" float-
ing between the long piers. A boom was
a string of logs in the water, like a float-
ing dock, which prevented the timber

from drifting out of the cove. One part of the boom was hinged to let logs in and out. Sometimes when it was very calm Davy was allowed to walk along the boom with his father. It was a little frightening because the way was narrow and the water around him very deep, but it was fun to watch the timber being stowed away on one of the sailing-ships that was anchored beside one of the square piers called a "block", in deep water beyond the boom.

Now, he was delighted to see some of the familiar sights again. "Papa," he said, "I can hardly wait to get home."

And Jacqueline added, "And I want to see Maman, and Madeleine, and Annette, and Willie. Come on, Davy, let's run."

CHAPTER 3

The Family

Like other houses along the river road, the Cameron house stood almost on the roadway itself with its back close to the cliffs that rose sharply behind it. It was of white roughcast and had a steep roof. At one side was a tiny yard and, at the other, a low shed for the chickens.

As they came near, the front door opened and Madeleine appeared.

"Maman, Maman, they're here!"

Mrs. Cameron came from the kitchen. Her black hair shone under her white linen cap. There were tears of joy in her dark brown eyes. It was such a long time since she had seen her two youngest children.

"*Ah, mes petits, mes petits!* [Oh my little ones, my little ones!]" she said as she kissed them and hugged them close to her. "It is so long! Look how you've grown, both of you, at Grand-mère's. Madeleine, take their toques and mufflers, and here, Annette, hang their coats on the pegs near the hearth."

Davy was so glad to be home that he didn't even mind that Maman called him "a little one".

Madeleine, who was eleven, and fair like her father, tweaked Davy's nose as she unfastened his muffler.

"Ouch," Davy squealed, and gave her a quick poke in the ribs.

Now it was Madeleine's turn to say "Ouch", but, before she could, Maman put out her hand and said, "Children! Children! Teasing already! Madeleine, don't you want to ask your brother about the Indians and what it was like out on the river?"

"Yes, Maman," Madeleine said obediently, but she gave Davy a secret look and thought, "It's fun to have someone to tease again."

Davy, who was not as tall as Madeleine but quite able to take care of himself, smiled at her as if to say, "I dare you." He began to tell her how it felt to be in the canoe when it was pulled up over the ice.

Maman, listening to their excited talk, thought again how much alike these two looked. Nodding towards them, she said to her husband, "They're like two peas in a pod."

"What are we having for dinner, Maman?" Davy asked. "I'm hungry."

"We're having all the things you like. Stew and dumplings and fresh bread and maple syrup."

"Oh, good!" he said. "Grand-mère makes good dumplings, too, but yours are the best."

Mrs. Cameron smiled and winked at Annette, who had made the dumplings this time. Annette was thirteen and could cook and sew almost as well as her mother. She continued setting the kitchen table and said nothing. She hoped that Davy would not be disappointed.

Davy, Jacqueline, and their father warmed their hands before the hot fire in the big stone fire-place where the dinner was cooking in a large iron pot. The pot hung over the fire on a long bar which was fastened into the side of the fire-place so that it could be moved back and forth. Mrs. Cameron swung the bar towards her, removed the pot, and filled the plates as the children brought them to her. Each carried his own to the table, Annette carried Papa's, and they sat down.

There was one empty place for Willie who, at seventeen, was the eldest of the family. Willie worked as a helper to a shipwright and, as they were very busy just now at the shipyards getting ready for the spring launchings, he was often late for dinner.

"We'll not wait for Willie, children," Mr. Cameron said and, signalling them

They loved this big brother.

to bow their heads, asked God's blessing on the good food that they were about to eat, and thanked Him for bringing them all safely together again.

Then Davy and Jacqueline picked up pieces of fluffy dumpling dripping with gravy and popped them into their mouths. They rolled their eyes and looked at Maman.

"Mm-mm! It's good," they said together.

Mrs. Cameron, pretending, said, "I don't think they're as good as usual today."

"Oh yes," Davy said. "They're better."

Then Annette could wait no longer and said, "But *I* made them." And everybody laughed.

In the midst of the laughter, Willie came in, stamping the wet snow off his boots. Davy and Jacqueline ran to him at once. They loved this big brother. He was almost as tall as Papa and had the round, happy face and black hair and eyes of their mother.

He lifted Jacqueline high in the air and then, putting his arm round Davy's shoulders, exclaimed, "And just look at *you*! What did Grand-mère feed you to make you grow so much?"

They all sat down again and listened while Willie told his father how the work on the new schooner was getting along.

"This one's going to be a beauty, Father," he said between mouthfuls. "They're putting the best into her — mahogany for the captain's cabin, and best-quality brass for the fittings and all. You should see her."

"I want to see her, too," Davy said. "Couldn't I go back with you after dinner?"

"Not today. We're very busy and there's no time for a young scamp like you always asking questions."

"I'll be as quiet as a mouse," Davy promised.

"You! Quiet as a mouse!" Willie teased. "'What's this for? How does that work? Why are they doing that?' That's how you'd be 'quiet as a mouse'. I know *you*. No, you can't come today, but maybe tomorrow after . . ."

Willie didn't get a chance to finish because Davy jumped up and threw his arms round his neck to show him how pleased he was.

As he looked at all their faces, Papa knew he had a fine family.

The next day was Sunday. It was only on Sunday that the Cameron family was divided. Mr. Cameron, a Scotsman, was a Presbyterian and Mrs. Cameron was French and a devout Roman Catholic. When they married, they agreed that they would stay with the faith in which they had been brought up. And, when they had children, they agreed that the boys would go to church with their father and the girls with their mother. It was not the best arrangement in the world but the Camerons made it work because they respected and loved each other.

So that Sunday morning Mrs. Cameron and the girls dressed in their best clothes and went off to Mass without breakfast, while Mr. Cameron and the boys ate their porridge alone and then started on the long walk to St. Andrew's Church on Ste. Anne Street in the Upper Town.

The weather had cleared and, although it was still cold, there was no wind. The path ran so close to the houses that by stretching out his arm Davy could have rapped on the window panes as he went by. He had often done it, and then run away. Should he try it now, just once? He was walking behind his father and started to stretch out his arm towards a window.

"Better not, Davy," his father said without turning around. "Or there'll be no visit to the schooner this afternoon."

Davy jerked his arm back as if he had touched something red-hot. He looked at his father's straight back in wonder and said to himself, "He must have eyes in the back of his head."

They walked on. It was a lovely day and he didn't feel a bit like being on his Sunday behaviour.

"Do you think Dr. Cook will preach a long time today, Willie?" he asked.

"Sure to, Davy lad."

"Dr. Cook preaches very good sermons," Mr. Cameron said, sternly. "If you'd pay more attention, you might learn a great deal."

"But I don't understand what he says."

His father frowned. What Davy said was true but Mr. Cameron thought the discipline of listening was good for him and he must learn to sit quietly and not grumble about it. "That's enough, Davy. We'll have no more talk about it."

When they came out of church, the sun shone brightly and the air was warmer. There was definitely a smell of spring to it, Davy thought as he sniffed it. "It will soon be time to watch for the first ship, won't it, Papa," he said excitedly.

It was a great event in Quebec when the ice had gone and the first ships arrived from across the ocean. Everyone looked forward to it.

They walked down Mountain Street past an old house, as they had done many times before. Over the doorway, it had a strange stone with a golden dog carved into it. The gold paint was almost all gone but Davy could make out the outlines of the dog and the verse which was written underneath in French.

I am a dog which gnaws a bone,
I crouch and gnaw it all alone —
A time will come, which is not yet,
When I'll bite him by whom I'm bit.

"Are there any real ghosts in there?" Davy asked, pretending that he wasn't afraid.

"That's what they say, though how a ghost could be real I don't know, I'm sure," Mr. Cameron said. "Some people believe they really see ghosts but I think it's all imagination."

"But they do say there's a curse on the place," Willie said. "Thomas O'Rourke, who works alongside of me, says he has seen lights flickering behind those broken shutters when he has been by late at night. And even the watch, going his rounds, crosses over to the other side of the street when he comes to it."

Mr. Cameron laughed. "Are you sure young Thomas hadn't been taking a drop too much, Willie? Now, *there's* a place you might well stay away from" — and he pointed to the Old Neptune Inn which they could just see at the foot of the hill. "Many a man has gone in there and never been heard of again. But whsst!" he said, noticing Davy's wide eyes, "we're frightening the boy. Let's hurry, or your mother will wonder what has become of us."

At that moment, Monsieur Le Blanc came out of the Old Neptune. Mr. Cameron gave a start. "This Monsieur Le Blanc keeps poor company," he said aside to Willie.

Davy shivered with a strange excitement. Monsieur Le Blanc's sharp, black eyes were staring right at him again.

CHAPTER 4

Watching for the
Spring Fleet

On the first day of May, the news came
to town that there were fifteen or
twenty ships, out of sight, beyond the
Traverse, waiting for a favourable
wind to sail up-river to Quebec.

Davy was at school when he heard
about the ships. At noon he came running home for his dinner. "Maman,
can't we go to the Terrace right away?
Do I have to go to school this afternoon?" he asked.

"Yes, Davy. You have to go to school.

But when school is out you may go and watch. The ships may not come today at all, you know."

Davy looked very disappointed but he knew that it was no use arguing with Maman. Papa and Maman thought school was very important and always paid the schoolmaster promptly. It cost a shilling and sixpence a month for each child, but, since it was the Protestant school, Davy was now the only one of the Cameron family who went there. Willie had left school three years before, to work. Annette stayed home to help her mother, and Madeleine and Jacqueline went to the school beside their parish church.

The whole class was restless that afternoon. Try as he would, Davy could not keep his mind on the six-times table, and, when the schoolmaster told him to read, he read a whole paragraph without understanding it.

The schoolmaster's name was Mr. Deacon, and, though he was a stern teacher, he was a kindly man. It was plain to him that the class was not going to learn very much today. He might as well let them go early.

Davy ran all the way home. "Can we go now, Maman?" he called as he came in the kitchen door.

"Yes, Davy. We will stop by for Jacqueline and Madeleine on the way." And she changed her linen cap for a bonnet, put her shawl around her shoulders, and took a few coins from the cracked cup on the shelf.

By the time they had climbed Mountain Street, they were out of breath from hurrying. They saw that a large crowd had already gathered on the Terrace.

"Are they in sight yet?" Davy asked an old man who was standing near the parapet.

"Not yet, my boy. But if an old sailor's any judge of weather, the wind's going to change soon. Here, would you like to get in front of me so you can see?"

Davy hesitated. He didn't want to miss the first sight of the ships, but Maman had promised to buy them some barley-sugar. He didn't want to miss that, either.

"Thank you, sir. I'll be back in a minute," he said.

He darted off between raftsmen in

brightly coloured shirts, soldiers of the garrison in red coats, and ladies in wide, hooped skirts and feathered bonnets. Maman had stopped beside an old woman who had gingerbread and barley-sugar sticks for sale on a tray.

"How much?" Maman asked.

"A penny for the gingerbread and big sugar sticks and halfpenny for the small ones, ma'am. And they're all fresh."

"All right, children," Maman said. "You may choose whatever you like."

"I'll take a big lemon one, please," Davy said at once.

"And I want a red one," Jacqueline piped up.

When the old woman had handed them over, Davy said, "Maman, there's a man over there who's saving a place

On the Terrace.

for me. See, he's looking this way."

The old sailor doffed his cap to Maman very politely as she came towards him. "The children will be safe with me, ma'am," he said.

"All right. Davy, you and Jacqueline may stay here. Annette and Madeleine and I will take a walk along the Terrace." The girls were pleased, because Maman was sure to meet some of her friends with their daughters and they would have a good visit.

The afternoon sun shone on the river far below but there was no sign of the spring fleet. Only the ferry to Lévis and some small craft could be seen.

Davy and Jacqueline would soon have become tired of watching if the old sailor had not been such a good story-teller. He told them about the many countries he had visited and about his adventures.

"And were you afraid when you saw the pirate ship?" Davy asked.

"Nope," the old man said. "I knew they'd never catch us. The *White Gull* was the fastest schooner on the seven seas, lad."

"Faster than a steamship, sir?"

"Steamship!" The old man fairly spat the word out. "Faster than a smelly, smoky, noisy old steamship? You bet she was. Steam'll never take the place of sail. Don't let anyone tell you different."

Davy remembered his father telling him about the steamship *Royal William* that was launched at Wolfe's Cove before he was born. He had said that it was a fine ship and all the people in the cove were proud because it was the first steamship to cross the ocean without using sails. And Mr. Deacon had said that some day all ships would use steam. But, since the old sailor had such a poor opinion of steamships, Davy said nothing.

Before long the wind changed, as the old man had said it would. A cry went up from the watchers on the Terrace when the first ship came in sight. It was followed by another, and then another, and soon there were twenty ships in full sail, heading towards the quays of Quebec.

What a pretty sight it was! Schooners, barques, brigantines! The first one docked and everyone cheered.

"It's the barque *Great Britain*," the

old sailor said. "I'd know her anywhere. Out of London, she is, and this is the third year in a row she's been first." He waved his cap and shouted, "Hurray for the *Great Britain!*"

"Hurray for the *Great Britain!*" Davy and Jacqueline shouted after him.

Now people were leaving the Terrace to go down the hill to see the ships close at hand. "Come children," Maman said, as she came up to them. "It is long past supper-time. Papa and Willie will be waiting."

"Maman, tell us Grand-père's story about the ships coming," Davy said as they walked along the road. And Maman told them how, during one spring when Grand-père was a little boy, there had not been enough to eat before the ships arrived. Davy had heard it all before but he liked to hear Maman tell how the ships brought flour and sugar and tea and all kinds of goods for shops that had become almost empty after the long, cold winter.

"Now," he said, "winter is really over, isn't it, Maman?"

"Yes, Davy, it is," she said with a smile.

CHAPTER 5

The Anxious Time

Mr. Cameron worked as Superintendent at Spencer Cove. Spring was his busiest time because the orders for timber had to be ready for loading on the sailing-ships that would take them to England.

He had to make sure that each piece was in good condition. If a piece had a bruised or split end, it was hauled up on the beach and Mr. Cameron would show one of the workmen where he wanted it trimmed and reshaped with the broad-axe. The discarded ends and chips kept the families of the cove in firewood and it was the regular job of the boys of the cove to go down after school with hand-carts and bring a load home.

Davy sometimes grumbled and said that he couldn't see how one family could use so much wood, but he didn't really mind this daily chore. With the other boys he would run out to the end of one of the piers and aim pebbles at the nearest ship anchored at one of the blocks.

One day, Davy made an extra-long throw which landed a pebble squarely in the middle of the back of a man who was handling a piece of timber with a pike-pole.

"You — you —!" the man roared towards them. "You little beasts get away from there or I'll get the crimps after you."

"You don't think he really would, do you, Davy?" one of the boys asked, as they ran off.

"Of course not," Davy answered. "We're too young. They just want the big boys." But he didn't waste any time getting away, for he remembered Monsieur Le Blanc and the man with the red beard.

This was the time of year the people of the coves called "the anxious time", because of the crimps.

"Papa," Davy asked that night at supper. "Why do you look so worried?"

Mr. Cameron touched the back of his hand to his forehead, as if to smooth away his worried look, and smiled. "Was I looking worried? It's nothing."

"I know. It's the crimps. You're afraid they'll get Willie, aren't you?"

"Hush," his father said sternly.

Willie pretended that there was nothing to be afraid of. "Don't you worry. I can take care of myself. See that muscle?" he said, pulling up his shirt-sleeve and flexing his arm.

"But if they hit you on the head, you won't have a chance to use it," Davy answered.

"Willie! Davy! We'll have no more talk about it," Mr. Cameron said sharply, and there was silence.

But after supper he took Willie aside. "A young fellow disappeared up at Sillery last night, Willie. They think it was the Chambers gang, but the police can do nothing about it, it seems. Be careful."

"I will. To tell you the truth, I'm more afraid of the cholera than of the crimps. The boy working with me lives in Lower Town and says there's talk of a case off the *Brigid O'Daniel.* It's a fearful thing the way it strikes you down so suddenly. Why, a man can be feeling fit as a fiddle today and be dead tomorrow!"

"I know. Pray God it won't be like it was in '34." He shuddered, remembering the sound of wooden carts going by at night and the cry of the drivers, "Bring out your dead!"

But, even during "the anxious time", there were pleasures and good times too. Davy never tired of seeing a new

Davy never tired of seeing a new ship launched.

ship launched, and there were many of them that year. School went on all through the summer except for two weeks. Sometimes, when it was very hot, Mr. Deacon would let them go early. Even if he did not, there was enough time after four o'clock to do many things during the long summer evenings.

Sometimes Davy would climb the hill to the Plains of Abraham to watch a cricket match. Sometimes, with the other boys, he would wander over to look at Wolfe's monument, which was almost falling to pieces. "Papa says it's a disgrace the way people chip bits off for souvenirs," he said. "He says there's talk of putting up a new one. I don't know why anyone would want to keep an old piece of stone." The boys agreed that stones were only good for throwing.

Davy knew all about the battle between the French and the British and when he was by himself he would sit at the foot of the monument and wonder what had happened to all the dead soldiers. Had they been buried there, where they fell, maybe right beneath his feet?

On Sunday afternoons they went walking on the Terrace. Maman and the girls would join them after church and they would have a picnic.

"Maman," he would say, "I like Sundays in the summer, best. You don't have to sit still all the time with nothing to do."

And his mother would look at his father out of the corner of her eye. Papa was not sure that coming here was quite the right thing to do on the Sabbath, but Maman thought it was not wrong to enjoy yourself, provided you had been to church first. So Papa let Maman have her way. He remembered that this was the only time in the week when she was free to do as she pleased. But in the winter they kept the quiet, Scottish Sabbath.

CHAPTER 6

Fire!

Near the end of June, Davy wakened one night to the sound of voices in the room he shared with Willie.

"It must be another bad one," Willie whispered, "to call on us again for help."

"I'm afraid it is. They say a whole street has gone already," his father said.

"What's gone?" Davy asked sleepily. There was no light in the room but he could see a glow in the sky.

"Hush, lad! Go back to sleep. There's

another fire. It's over in the St. John district this time. Willie and I are going over with the fire brigade to help put it out."

Davy was wide awake now. "Can't I come?"

"No. It's no place for a child," he said.

In the morning, Mr. Cameron and Willie were still not home. Mrs. Cameron was worried until a neighbour, Monsieur Duval, called to say that they were all right.

"Is the fire out yet?" Mrs. Cameron asked him in French.

"No, madame. We put it out in one place and it springs up in another." Monsieur Duval looked very tired.

"I will take the men some food. Where shall I find them?"

"Go to Ste. Anne and Ste. Ursule streets, madame. You will be safe there and they will try to come there in an hour. *Misère*! What a fire! It is as bad as the St. Roch fire last month. Listen!" There was the sound of an explosion. "They're blowing up two or three houses to stop the fire from spreading into the St. Louis district."

Mrs. Cameron put cheese, bread, a bottle of wine, a flask of water, and some linen for bandages in a basket. "Davy, you may go with me," she said, handing it to him. This was one time she would allow him to miss school. A boy might be of more help than one of the girls, to run an errand or to take a message.

They started off. Great clouds of black smoke hung over the city, and as they came nearer they could see flames shooting up into the sky. Everyone they met carried a bundle of clothes or household goods saved from the fire.

"Maman, look! There's a man pushing a cart with so many things on it, I don't know how they stay on at all. I can see chairs and a bedstead and a cradle and . . ." Just then an iron pot fell with a great clatter on the cobblestones. Davy picked it up and handed it to the man, but he could find no place to put it on the loaded cart.

"Would you carry it for me, son?" he asked. "I'm not going much farther — only to my brother's house on Mountain Street."

Davy looked at his mother. She nodded. "I'll wait here till you get back. Only hurry." And they disappeared across the square into the crowd.

Davy was back in ten minutes. "Maman," he said, "the man told me that many people just managed to escape in the clothes they had on and lots of them have nowhere to go and are camping out in the fields. He said the fire started in a wooden house and there ought to be a law against wooden houses and . . ." He stopped for breath as they hurried to the place where Monsieur Duval had told them to wait.

The fire seemed very close now. A fire-engine went rushing by as fast as the horses could gallop and people scattered in all directions to get out of its way. In the distance, they could hear the roar of the flames above the shouting of the men and the snorting of frightened horses. They could feel the heat come towards them in waves. Dense clouds of smoke and cinders swept down upon them from time to time.

"Will it burn the whole city?" he asked.

"No. They will surely put it out soon," his mother answered, but she looked very worried.

In a few minutes, they saw Willie and Mr. Cameron walking wearily towards them. Their faces were black with soot and Willie was holding one arm. As they came nearer, Davy could see that Willie's arm was bleeding.

"Willie," he called, running towards him. "Are you hurt?"

"It's nothing much. A bit of glass caught me when a window of a burning house blew out."

Mrs. Cameron bathed Willie's arm with water from the flask and bandaged it. They moved to a quiet side street. The men sat down on a doorstep and ate slowly, too tired to talk. They were just finishing when they heard a cry of "Help!"

"Where did that come from?" Mr. Cameron said, jumping to his feet.

"Back here," Willie said. "That's queer. The fire's not that way. Listen, there it is again!"

"Help! Help!"

Willie, with Davy at his heels, and Mr. Cameron following, ran towards the sound. Half-way down the narrow street an even narrower alley turned off at a right-angle. They saw, in the alley a few yards away, a limp figure being dragged off quickly by two men.

They saw a limp figure being dragged off.

"Stop!" Willie cried. "Stop! What are you doing?"

Davy, rushing ahead of him, shouted "They're crimps!"

The men took one look backwards, let go of their victim, ran to the end of the alley, and disappeared over a fence. Davy had recognized one of them. "It was Redbeard," he said, as his father joined them and they came to the man on the ground. "You know, one of the men who met Monsieur Le Blanc that day we came home from Grand-mère's."

"Are you sure, Davy?"

"Yes, Papa. I'm sure. I couldn't ever forget the way he looked at me — as if he wanted to hit *me* over the head like he did this one."

The man on the ground groaned and opened his eyes. Terrified, he tried to get up. "Crimps," he thought, and then, realizing that the faces bending over him were kind, he sank back and said weakly, "Who are you?"

"We heard your cry for help," Mr. Cameron said, "and came as quickly as we could. What happened?"

The man sat up and rubbed his head. "Far as I can remember, I was just settin' there on that step, dozin' on account of bein' up all night fightin' the fire, and first thing I know these two fellows are tryin' to tie me up. I yelled and kicked and knocked one of 'em over and then the other hit me on the head, I guess. Anyhow, that's all I remember till I see you bendin' over me. I'm that grateful to you, I can't say how much, sir."

"Never mind that. Who were they?"

Mr. Cameron asked.

"Never saw 'em before in my life."

"Too bad," Mr. Cameron said. "I hoped you might know."

Later in the day the wind changed and the men gradually put out the fire. More than 1,000 houses had been burned.

CHAPTER 7

A Narrow Escape

One hot afternoon in August, when he was on holidays, Davy and his friend Pierre Duval sat swinging their legs over the edge of a pier wondering what to do.

"Let's go exploring," Pierre said.

"We've explored everywhere around here," Davy answered.

"I know one place we haven't been," Pierre whispered. "The old Palace."

"Oh, but we can't go there. We're forbidden to go through the Lower

Town alone. Papa says it's full of drunken sailors — maybe crimps, even!" Davy's eyes shone with excitement.

"Are you scared to go?"

"N . . . no. Only if Papa ever found out he'd give me a good whipping."

"My father would too, but nobody needs to know. I dare you!"

They started off, hands in pockets, whistling and kicking up the dust as if going nowhere in particular. By the time they reached the Lower Town they felt quite brave. It was too hot for many people to be about and those they saw paid no attention to them at all. They went down to the waterfront and wandered out on the government wharf to see what was going on. Ships were loading and unloading and everybody was very busy, but they had seen it all before.

"Come on," Davy said. "Let's go. It feels like a thunder-storm."

They followed the narrow streets below the ramparts till they came to the Queen's woodyard. Parts of it had been cleared out since the first big fire of that year, but over by the old Palace where coal had been stored wisps of smoke still rose here and there among the ruins.

"Look!" Davy said. "There's nothing left of the old walls, at all — just heaps of stones."

"Papa brought me here once," Pierre said. "He told me stories of the old days of New France when fine ladies and gentlemen came in their carriages to see the Intendant and there were lights in all the windows. It was beautiful then, before you English destroyed it with your guns."

"They weren't *my* guns," Davy protested. "You've got an English grandfather yourself. Anyway, it was all so long ago, who cares?"

Pierre shrugged. He hadn't meant to offend his friend. "Papa cares," he said. "But never mind. We'd better go home before they miss us."

"And before it rains," Davy added. "Look how black it's getting!"

But even though the sky was dark and there was a distant roll of thunder the boys couldn't resist taking time to look in shop windows as they went along. There were so many interesting things to see —all kinds of gear and supplies for ships and rafts, and trinkets to tempt a sailor or raftsman to part with a few shillings.

Suddenly, there was a loud clap of thunder and it began to rain. At first, it came slowly in big drops that spattered noisily on the cobblestones but, in a moment, it poured, carried forward by the wind in great sheets.

"Quick!" Davy cried. "Get in this doorway, Pierre."

"No, over here, Davy. It looks like an old warehouse and we can go inside till it's over." Pierre tried the door as he spoke and it opened.

Curiously, the boys looked around them. The only windows in the long, low room were two small dormers set in the roof on the far side. Davy tiptoed over while Pierre looked into some boxes and casks.

"This isn't a warehouse, Pierre. It's a loft. See, the hill slopes away and there's a lower floor that opens on the street below. I think there's a shop below us."

As he spoke, a door banged and they heard voices.

"Maybe we shouldn't be here," Pierre whispered. It was a creepy place in the half-darkness with the thunder rumbling overhead.

"Nobody will know, if we're quiet," Davy said. "And we can't go out in this rain."

They stood very still listening to every sound. The voices, though not the words, could be heard above the noise of the storm. They were loud and quarrelling.

Davy motioned to Pierre to follow

him towards a thin sliver of light that showed through the floor. When he reached it, he found that it came through a knot-hole and, kneeling quietly, he peered down. He seemed to be looking into a small room lit by candles on a table directly beneath him. Suddenly, he gasped and clapped his hand over his mouth.

"What is it?" Pierre whispered.

"Sh-sh! It's Redbeard."

"Who's he?"

"You know. The one I told you about. Sh-sh! Listen!"

An angry voice came through clearly. "I tell you, Le Blanc, now's the time to get rid of that one. He has made too much trouble already. If the skipper of the *Skylark* will pay £50 for him, *I* say take it."

"Aye, aye," said two other voices together.

At that there was a crash as if someone had banged on the table. "Silence!" roared Monsieur Le Blanc. He stepped into the light, and Davy could see him now. "*I'm* the one who says what'll be done around here and you'd better remember it if you don't want to end up in the river. That one's a *real* sailor — none of your riff-raff. He's worth more than £50."

There was a sullen look on Redbeard's face as he said, "All right, all right. No need to get upset, Le Blanc. We'll keep him up country till you're ready. What's next?"

"Two men off the *Silver Snipe* have registered at Pension Mornay, Red. Bring them over to the Old Lion Inn and get them drunk. Then Harry and Jacques, here, will take over. In the meantime, boys," (he faced the other two who were in the shadows) "see what you can find along the shore between here and St. Michael's Cove. The *Skylark* will take six if we can get them. But no stiffs! The skipper said he'd turn us in if we handed him a dead one again."

Davy's eyes became bigger and bigger. Pierre was holding his hands over his mouth and looked terrified. The storm was passing now and it had become quiet in the loft.

Redbeard spoke again. "Skippers are getting mighty sore-headed these days, Le Blanc. Like old Duffus of the *Blue Heron*. He says he comes into port with this good crew and first thing he knows, they've most of 'em deserted. He says as how honest fellows like us has something to do with it, he does." Red laughed and the others joined in. "Then, mind you, he says the crew we got for him last time — out of the goodness of our hearts, boys — well, he says they near run him aground down in the gulf." Red slapped his thigh and laughed again.

Pierre motioned to Davy to let him have a look. Carefully, he knelt down and put his face close to the dusty floor.

Le Blanc said, "That's his look-out. Old Duffus had better not complain to anybody else, that's all. He's just the kind that might, too — not properly scared of us at all. We may have to shut him up yet. All right boys, let's go. The usual place tomorrow night, eleven o'clock. If anything goes wrong, I'll be here till half past ten."

Suddenly, Pierre sneezed. Horrified, the boys froze and listened.

"What was that?" said Le Blanc sharply.

"The wind. You're jumpy today, Le Blanc."

"Did you lock that door upstairs last time you went out that way, Harry?"

"Sure I did. Like he says, you're jumpy."

The boys breathed more freely. But, in a moment, Pierre felt it coming again. He tried his best to choke it off and Davy, trying to help, reached over to put his hands over Pierre's mouth. He sneezed again.

Monsieur Le Blanc sprang to his feet. "There *is* someone upstairs," he

The boys were already half-way to the door.

shouted as he made for a ladder leading to the trap-door to the loft.

The boys now had but one thought — to get out of there as fast as their legs would carry them. As the head and shoulders of Monsieur Le Blanc pushed up through the trap-door, the boys were already half-way to the outside door. "If that door sticks, we're goners," Davy thought as he ran across the rough boards. His hands found the latch and he pulled. It opened and, with Pierre at his heels, he ran into the street and off towards home.

At first, Monsieur Le Blanc ran after them. But his shoes slipped on the wet cobblestones, and he stumbled. The boys were far ahead. He gave up and went back to his shop.

Davy and Pierre didn't stop running

until they were well down the river road.

"Whew!" Davy panted. "That was close."

"Do you think they know who we are?" Pierre asked.

"They wouldn't know you, Pierre, but, even though they only saw our backs, Redbeard and old Le Blanc would know *me*. *I'd* know *them* anywhere — back or front."

Pierre replied, "Anyway, they don't know where you live, Davy."

Davy felt somewhat relieved at that. "I wonder what time it is and if we're late for supper. And what are we going to tell them at home if we are?"

"We'll just tell them we got caught in the rain and took shelter — which is what we did," Pierre said.

"And not say anything to anyone about what we heard?"

"We can't," Pierre said. "We weren't supposed to be there. And anyway, what *do* we know?"

"We know they're crimps and they're planning something for tomorrow night."

Pierre thought things out for a moment. He was remembering that his father hit very hard when he was angry. And he would be angry all right if he found out that he had been disobeyed. Finally, he said, "But we don't know where the crimps were going to meet. The police would never believe us if we couldn't tell them that. They'd say we were just making up a story."

"Monsieur Le Blanc said he would be there, at his shop or whatever it is, until half past ten. The police could get *him*," Davy said.

"Police couldn't arrest a man just for being in his own shop at night."

"I guess you're right, Pierre. It wouldn't do any good to tell anyone and we'd only get punished."

They parted at Pierre's door. "Remember, Davy," he warned. "Not a word! We were down by the shipyards and took shelter from the storm."

Davy nodded and went on home.

CHAPTER 8

Two for the Crimps

Autumn came and the sumacs that clung to the steep sides of the heights along the river road turned scarlet. Nearly 1,500 ships had come and gone at Quebec that year, some with men below decks securely bound and gagged until they were out of sight of the city. Only when the last ship sailed down the river would "the anxious time" come to an end for another year.

"Father," Willie said one morning in September, "would it take a man very long to learn to design the ships we build at the yards?"

"It might," his father answered. "And then again, if a man had the knack of it and knew mathematics and such things, it might not. Why do you ask?"

"I've been thinking. I've no mind to be a ship's carpenter all my life."

"It's a good trade."

"Yes, but some day they'll not be building sailing-ships any more and there'll be new ways of doing things and I want to know about them. Then, when my chance comes, I'll be able to take it."

"Then you had better go back to school and learn what's necessary. We can hardly spare your wages, but if you're set on getting an education I'll not stop you."

"I could learn at night. Mr. Deacon would teach me. I met him along the road the other day and asked him if he would, provided you were willing, of course."

Mr. Cameron looked at his son. He was proud that he wanted to better himself. He smiled. "I see it's all settled then, Willie, and I'm pleased."

Davy, who hadn't been paying much attention until he heard the schoolmaster's name, looked puzzled. "I can't see why you want to go to school when you don't have to. When I grow up, I'm going to be a raftsman. You don't have to go to school to be a raftsman do you, Papa?"

"No, Davy. You don't have to have much book-learning for that but you have to learn a lot of other things and it's a hard life. Wouldn't you like to be a schoolmaster like Mr. Deacon?"

Davy shook his head. He didn't like lessons. You had to sit still and listen when you wanted to be outside, running along the piers or clambering over half-finished ships. "No, Papa," he said. "If I can't be a raftsman I'd rather work with Willie in the shipyard or with you at the cove."

"Well, there's plenty of time to think of that," he smiled.

Willie added: "There's time, but you'd better learn your lessons when you've got the chance — that is, if you want to grow up to be smart like your brother." And he winked at him across the table.

When Willie got up to go, Maman took him aside and whispered. "But Willie, you'll be coming home after dark."

"Don't worry. The ships will soon be all gone. We won't have to fear the crimps much longer."

Maman was not satisfied. She looked worried. "That's just the time to be careful," she said.

"I'll be careful," he answered.

Every night after supper now, Willie went to the schoolmaster's house to learn mathematics and Latin for the sum of a shilling a week. Davy, who thought that everything Willie did was right, made up his mind to do his best and get good marks. He wanted Willie to be proud of him.

The Camerons began to get ready for winter. After school each day Davy brought loads of wood from the cove and piled them in the woodshed. When the shed was filled, he piled them against the back of the house. The other boys whose fathers worked at the cove did the same and soon the beaches were almost cleared of the pieces of discarded logs.

Although there were still logs within the boom, the coves were beginning to look empty. Later on, some of the unsold logs would be brought up on the beach and the damaged ones would be sold cheaply for firewood. The biggest pieces would be pushed to the back of the fire-place where they would burn slowly throughout the long winter nights.

"Next year, Maman, we will buy a stove," Papa said one cold October morning. "It will keep us warmer and it will be easier for you to cook on than the fire-place. They say some of them have very good ovens now."

"Now, Papa," she answered, "I would not know how to manage a stove. If it smoked, I would not know what to do and, as for the oven, do you think my bread and biscuits would be any better baked there than in this fine brick oven in the wall of the fire-place?"

"Of course not, Maman. I just wanted to make things easier for you."

Maman looked pleased at that. "Thank you, but this is the way I've always done things and I'm content — for the present, anyway." After all, she might want to change her mind some day. She was proud that she had never had to go to the neighbours for a shovel of coals to start the morning fire. Madame Simon who lived next door was always letting her fire go out and having to borrow coals.

Mr. Cameron dug a pit in the pebbly ground beside the house and into it they put carrots and potatoes and turnips. In the middle, they put a length of pipe to let air in and then they covered the vegetables with sand. In that way, they would keep fresh most of the winter.

Madeleine and Jacqueline peeled apples and Annette quartered them and threaded a cord through each piece with a big needle. Then they hung them from the ceiling near the fireplace to dry. Long after the fresh apples had begun to wither, these dried ones would be delicious when Maman boiled them and sweetened them with maple sugar. In another part of the kitchen

Maman hung bunches of herbs to dry for the seasoning of soups and stews. Davy loved the sweet, spicy smell of the kitchen, these autumn days.

Because there was no room for a garden between their house and the cliffs, Maman bought most of these things at the market. One night at supper she would say to Davy, "Tomorrow we will go early to market. It is the best time to buy apples." And the next morning she would wake him before dawn and he would take his little cart to be loaded with food to be put away for the winter. Then they would return in time for Davy to go to school.

One day in November, when Mr. Cameron came home for dinner, he looked unusually cheerful. "Well,

Maman, we are loading the last ship today. I think she's the last ship loading at any of the coves, too. Tonight she'll be ready to sail, though she'll probably not move out till dawn tomorrow. Then, no more worries for another year!"

Maman smiled. "Le Bon Dieu is good to us," she said. "I shall go to Mass tomorrow morning and thank Him."

But that evening when Willie came home to supper, Maman looked worried.

"What's the matter, Maman?" he asked at once. And then he saw that the couch had been drawn up near the fire and that Jacqueline, looking very dull-eyed and feverish, was lying on it.

His mother nodded towards her. "The Sisters sent her home from school early this afternoon because she wasn't feeling well. But she'll be all right soon," she said, giving her daughter an encouraging smile. She drew Willie aside and whispered. "She has quite a high fever, I think. I was just wondering if I should send for the doctor."

"I could stop in at his house tonight on my way to the schoolmaster's and ask him to come if you like. What do you think is the matter with her?"

"I don't know, Willie. She looks — different — oh, it's probably just the grippe. We'll see how she is after supper."

After supper Jacqueline was the same. "I think she'll be all right, Willie," Maman said. "She's coughing now and

I'm putting mustard on her chest. I only wish your father hadn't gone to the meeting at the church. We might need him here. But you run along."

"If you change your mind, Maman, you could send Davy."

"After dark! Oh, I wouldn't like to do that, Willie."

"He would be all right, Maman. Everything's quiet now."

Willie knew that his mother didn't like Davy to hear the rough talk of the men who came out of the taverns and walked the river road at night. "Anyway," he said. "I hope you won't have to." He waved good-bye to Jacqueline and hurried off to the schoolmaster's house.

He did well with his Latin and with the first two problems in algebra but he found the third one very difficult. Mr. Deacon spent a good deal of time explaining it and had him work at similar problems until he understood them. Therefore it was later than usual when the schoolmaster closed his book.

"Tomorrow we might start geometry," he said. "I think you're about ready for that now."

"Thank you, sir. Good-night, sir," Willie said and he started to put on his coat.

Just then, there was a knock at the door. Mr. Deacon opened it. "Why Davy," he said. "What are you doing here? Come in."

"Maman sent me to get the doctor for Jacqueline, Mr. Deacon. I stopped by but he wasn't at home so I came on for Willie."

Willie, who had followed Mr. Deacon through the little passageway, said, "How is she, Davy?"

"She can hardly breathe," he answered. "I ran all the way."

"Did they say at the doctor's house where he was or how long he would be gone?"

"They said he had gone to see someone in the big house on the upper road and they would tell him about Jacqueline as soon as he got back. What shall we do now, Willie?"

Willie looked at the schoolmaster. "I think I should go after him, don't you, sir?"

"Yes, I think you should. It sounds as if the little girl is pretty sick. Davy, would you like to wait here with me until Willie gets back?"

"No, sir. That is, thank you, sir, but I'd like to go with Willie."

The schoolmaster nodded. "That's all right. Good-night, boys. And good luck to you!"

It was one of those gusty autumn nights when clouds move heavily across the sky. They hid the moon and occasionally brought short showers of rain. On the river, the ship that had been loading at the block rode at anchor. Her lights bobbed ceaselessly when the wind roughened the water and then nodded gently when it died down.

At any other time, those twinkling lights would have reminded Willie of danger. But tonight, with Davy running along beside him, he was thinking of his errand and the sick child at home. The river road was quiet as they came to the path which led to the heights above.

They were just turning into it when three men jumped on them. One man wrapped his arm round Willie's throat and pulled him backwards. Willie lashed out wildly with arms and feet at the second man. "Run, Davy," he gasped. The second man tied a gag across Willie's mouth. When Willie saw the third man catch hold of Davy he struggled furiously and almost broke loose. Then one of the men hit him on the head and knocked him out.

Davy fought. As the third man tried to tie a gag over his mouth, Davy bit him and kicked him in the shins. The man swore, tightened the gag, and

Three men jumped on them.

knocked the wind out of him with a
punch in the stomach. Davy punched,
scratched, and kicked. It was no use.
They tied him up like a mummy. He
could not see or move, but he could
hear.

"We weren't expecting this one," one
man said. "What shall I do with him?"

And a voice that sounded familiar to Davy answered: "Take him out to the boat and let Number One have the say of that. We can't leave him here to give us away, that's sure. Go off now and look for other stragglers."

Then Davy knew. It was Redbeard and he was caught. He felt himself being lifted over a fence.

CHAPTER 9

The Chase

After the boys had left, Mr. Deacon stayed at the door for a few moments and then turned back into the house. As he went over to the table he noticed that Willie had forgotten his Latin book.

The schoolmaster opened the door and looked out. For a brief moment the clouds parted and the moon shone full on the river road. What Mr. Deacon saw in the distance was not two figures walking quietly along the road, but several, struggling together.

In a flash, he understood what was happening. "My walking-stick! Quickly! And the poker!" he shouted to his wife as he rushed into the kitchen.

He ran out of the house and down the road, banging on each door with the poker as he went along, crying, "Help! The crimps!"

He could not wait to see if his cries roused anyone, but he knew that if he were heard the whole neighbourhood would come to his aid. If only they were in time, he thought, for the sky had darkened and he couldn't see anyone in the road ahead.

As he neared the spot where he had seen the men struggling, lights were beginning to appear in the houses he had passed. Behind him, a man stuck his head out of a window.

"What's going on?" he shouted. "Someone yelled 'the crimps'."

Mr. Deacon shouted back at him, "They've got Willie Cameron and young Davy, too. Hurry!"

Fenced in between the road and the river at this point were several low, frame buildings, uneven piles of cordwood and discarded logs. "Good cover for a quick get-away," Mr. Deacon muttered to himself. "Where shall I look first?"

He hesitated. He was brave, but he was small and no longer strong, and he felt helpless. Then, listening intently to every sound, he heard unmistakably the squeak of an oar in an oar-lock. The crimps were rowing out to the ship through the cove.

Just then three men who had been

aroused by his knocking came towards him. He called to them. "One of you go and get the boys' father and anyone else you can. Tell them to make for the ship. And to bring arms!"

As they stumbled in the dark towards the beach, one of the two men who were left said bitterly, "Willie's my friend, Mr. Deacon. I could kill those devils."

The schoolmaster recognized a neighbour and his son John. "First we need a boat," he said.

"Look! Over here! Here's a boat!" John called. And then, as he jumped in, "But there are no oars!"

By this time other men had appeared, some carrying lanterns with candles in them.

"Quickly!" the schoolmaster called. "We must find oars. Search those buildings and break in, if necessary."

One of the men found two pairs of oars leaning against the wall of a shed.

The schoolmaster, John and his father, and Mr. Brennan, a big Irishman who said that he was "mighty handy with his fists", set off at once. The others went to look for another boat.

Though they could see no sign of the crimps ahead of them, they rowed towards the ship's lights. Grimly, John and the schoolmaster pulled on the oars.

They were nearing the ship when they heard a pistol shot.

"I can see them," Mr. Brennan, who was in the bow, cried. "To the right! But keep low."

There was another shot, poorly

aimed, but the flash of the powder showed exactly where the boat was and, with a few strokes, the rescuers pulled alongside.

Mr. Brennan leapt aboard, brought the poker down hard on the first head he came to, and knocked the pistol out of Redbeard's hand as he was trying to re-load it. Redbeard tried to push the Irishman overboard, but somehow he kept his balance long enough for John's father to attack from behind, throw him face down over the seat, and sit on him.

"Be careful for the boys," Mr. Brennan shouted as he made for the third man who crouched in the stern. What he could not see was that this one had a knife. As he sprang, the crimp thrust it deep into his shoulder.

Mr. Brennan brought the poker down hard.

With a shout of pain, Mr. Brennan grabbed him by the throat. Using all the power of his right arm in one violent effort, he forced the crimp to the floorboards and held him there.

John and the schoolmaster had been holding the two boats together to keep them steady. Now, John stepped into the other boat and cut the bonds of the two boys.

Davy sat up, rubbing his wrists and ankles where the ropes had hurt them. His teeth were chattering with cold and fright, and for once he could not say a word. John wrapped his coat around him and handed him over to the schoolmaster. But Willie lay still.

During the short fight, there had been no sign of life on the ship near by. Now, however, figures appeared at the rail and a voice called, "Ho, there! What's going on?"

"We're men from the cove," Mr. Deacon shouted. "And we've caught the crimps bringing two of our boys to your ship."

There was silence for a moment. Then the voice came again. "We don't know anything about it. Take 'em ashore." And the figures promptly disappeared.

"They'd have taken Willie and Davy all right if we hadn't saved them," the schoolmaster said angrily.

During the fight Mr. Cameron came to the beach. Someone had already found another boat and he leapt in quickly as they were about to push off. "Hurry, I heard a shot," he said.

At the second shot, Mr. Cameron

shouted, "Faster, faster!" to the men who were already putting every ounce of strength into the rowing. Somehow, they did go faster and Mr. Cameron sat tensely in the bow, gun at the ready in his hand.

In a short time they could make out the other boats. A voice rang out. "Don't shoot. We've got them but we need help. Come alongside."

"Where are the boys? Are they all right?" were Mr. Cameron's first words as the three boats came together.

Davy, still shivering, poked his head over the side and cried, "P-p-papa! We're s-safe!"

"But where's Willie?" his father asked.

"He's lying in the bow," said the schoolmaster. "I don't know how badly he's hurt. Mr. Brennan has been knifed and is bleeding, but he's holding his man. We need help tying these fellows up."

"P-papa, look! It's Monsieur Le Blanc!" Davy cried, looking for the first time at the man Mr. Brennan was holding. There, staring at him in the light of the lantern, was Le Blanc.

"He's the ringleader, Mr. Cameron," Mr. Brennan said bitterly. "I've suspected him before this."

Hardly looking at Le Blanc, Mr. Cameron tied him up securely.

He carefully made his way towards Willie. "Willie, lad! What have they done to you?" he said. But there was no reply. He took his son's hand. It was cold. He put his ear to his chest and listened for his heartbeat. Yes, his son was alive, at least.

"Hurry! We must get him to a doctor," he said, looking up. "And you, Mr. Brennan. You're in bad shape. How can I ever thank you for what you've done this night?"

"Anyone would have done it, Mr. Cameron. I just wish we could get all the crimps as easily as we got this lot."

"We will yet, Mr. Brennan. We will yet."

They rowed the boats back to shore, and took the crimps to the police.

CHAPTER 10

Happy New Year!

On New Year's Eve the Cameron family sat beside the kitchen fire, talking about the night of the crimps. When the doctor had finally come to see Jacqueline, he had found two other patients waiting for him at the Cameron house — Willie and Mr. Brennan. He had bound up Mr. Brennan's wound and sent him home with orders to go to bed and stay there for a day or two until he had recovered from the loss of blood. Jacqueline, he had told them, had pneumonia, and Willie had a bad concussion. "And this young fellow," the doctor had said, putting his hand on Davy's shoulder, "has got off with a bad scare."

"Well, I guess I was just a little bit scared," Davy had admitted.

The doctor had ordered Jacqueline and Willie to stay in bed, and Mrs. Cameron or Annette had brought them all their food on trays. Within a month they were both well again, and able to go outside.

Tonight there was an air of expectancy in the room, for they were waiting for the band of singers called *Les Guignoleux* to knock on the door. On the table were gifts which the singers would collect to give to the poor. There were warm mittens, mufflers, and stockings knit by Mrs. Cameron and the girls, and a rag doll which Jacqueline had made all by herself while she was getting better.

Besides the gifts there were refreshments for the singers — squares of choice, spiced pork, biscuits, and wine.

Davy sat on a footstool beside Willie. There was a close, happy feeling between them, for they had shared a dangerous adventure and come through it safely together.

Willie tousled Davy's hair playfully. "Well, Davy, we're the lucky ones. I wonder where I'd be tonight if . . ." He stopped because Maman looked upset.

But Davy went on, "And I wonder what they would really have done with me."

"Come now," said Papa. "We've talked about it all before. Let's forget it for tonight, shall we?"

Just then there came a rapping on the door in time to the rhythm of a song which they all knew well.

"Here they are!" said Davy as he ran to open the door.

The family followed him, saying together, "Come in and welcome this New Year's Eve!"

Fifteen or more young people entered without pausing in their song. They sang in French:

Good-day to you, master and mistress
And all good people of the house.
We have made a promise
To come to see you once a year.
Once a year is not much.
Just a little piece of pork,
A little piece of pork
If you like;

If you have nothing to give us
Just say so.
We will take the eldest girl,
And roast her feet for her,

And here, Annette pretended to be alarmed.

Quickly, Mr. and Mrs. Cameron handed the plate of pork around to the singers, pretending to hurry so that Annette would not "get her feet roasted". Then everyone laughed.

Davy passed the biscuits, which were a special kind made of flour, sugar, and spice, and a tiny glass of wine was offered to each singer.

They admired the gifts. "Oh, what fine stockings," they said. "And the mittens and mufflers, too. We need so many things this year because many people lost everything they had in the great fires last summer."

One of the girls picked up the rag doll. "Very pretty, indeed!"

"I made it all myself," Jacqueline said, pleased with herself.

"I'll give it to the nicest little girl I can find," the girl said, smiling at her.

Then the singers gathered round Willie and Davy and sang a song which they had made up themselves. "There were two brothers who got caught by the crimps", it began, and it went on to praise their courage and to tell how they had been rescued.

Davy was delighted but Willie looked embarrassed. "But *I* didn't do anything. It was all the others who went after me. *I* was only stupid enough to let myself get caught. Here is one of the real

Then the singers gathered round.

heroes of that night." And he pulled his friend from the crowd. "And the schoolmaster and all the others who helped to capture old Le Blanc and his gang," he added.

At that, the crowd cried, "Never mind, Willie. You fought hard till they hit you. Anyone who gets away from the crimps is a hero." The singers danced round the three of them in the crowded kitchen.

"Come along with us on our rounds, Willie," they cried when they had finished.

"Take me, too! Please!" Davy whispered excitedly in Willie's ear.

Willie smiled. "All right, come along." And they began to put on their coats.

Then one of the singers said, "One

more song, my friends, and this one is especially for the head of this household." They began:

> *Should auld acquaintance be forgot*
> *And never called to mind,*
> *We'll drain the cup of friendship, yet,*
> *For auld lang syne.*

They sang the words in English but the accents that blended together in the words of the lovely old Scottish song were French, English, Irish, and Scottish, like the people who sang them.